They think that nothing can happen because they've shut the door.
—Maeterlinck

To the children who were arrested in July 1942,
and to Claude Roy—and Loleh—
who never forgot them.

STAR OF FEAR, STAR OF HOPE

Jo Hoestlandt

Illustrations by Johanna Kang

Translated from the French by Mark Polizzotti

SCHOLASTIC INC.

New York   Toronto   London   Auckland   Sydney

ISBN 0-590-86467-X

Text copyright © 1993 by Editions Syros.
English translation copyright © 1995 by Mark Polizzotti.
All rights reserved. Published by Scholastic Inc., 555 Broadway, New York, NY 10012, by arrangement with Walker Publishing Company, Inc.

12 11 10 9 8 7 6 5 4 3 2 1   6 7 8 9/9 0 1/0

Printed in the U.S.A.   08

First Scholastic printing, September 1996

My name is Helen, and I'm nearly an old woman now. When I'm gone, who will remember Lydia? That is why I want to tell you our story.

In 1942, the north of France was invaded by the German army. Neither the war nor the Germans could keep Lydia and me from going to school, or playing together, or getting into fights and making up, the way friends do all over the world.

One day, while we were playing nearby, Lydia's mother sewed a yellow star onto Lydia's jacket.

I said, "What a pretty star."

Lydia's mother answered, "Pretty or not, we have no choice. Every Jew must wear it. It's the new law."

Lydia's mother finished sewing on the star. "The place for stars is in the sky," she said. "When people take them down from the sky and sew them on their clothes, it only brings trouble."

She broke the white thread with a sharp pull of her teeth and said, "Stars at morning, better take warning. Stars at night, hope is in sight. So let's hope . . ."

I could see they were worried about these stars, so I stopped talking about them. I even stopped thinking about them.

Until one day.

It was July 15, 1942, and I was very happy because the next day, July 16, I would be nine years old. Since it was a special occasion, Lydia had permission to sleep over at my house. We were there all alone.

My father and mother didn't come home until midnight. They worked in a noisy bar where Papa played piano and Mama was a waitress. She always had to smile to keep the customers happy. By the end of the evening, her mouth hurt from so much smiling!

That night, Lydia and I were telling each other scary stories about zombies to see if our hair would stand on end, like in the comic books.

Suddenly we heard someone coming up the stairs. Strange—usually everyone was asleep at that hour. The sound of footsteps came right by my door. Lydia and I could feel our hearts beating very fast.

I got up, with Lydia right behind me, to make sure the door was locked—it was (whew!). Then I peeked through the keyhole.

A woman was standing at the door across the hall, scratching on it like a cat. She kept saying, "Open up, it's Madam Eleven O'Clock. Open up, it's Madam Eleven O'Clock."

No one answered. I looked at the clock. It was a quarter to eleven.

"What's she doing?" Lydia asked.

"Nothing," I said. "She has a star just like yours, and she's pulling at it. She looks like she doesn't know *what* to do."

Suddenly we heard more footsteps on the stairway. Madam Eleven O'Clock fled to the top floor in fear.

The footsteps stopped at my door. This time I let Lydia look through the keyhole.

"It's a big man with a red face," she whispered. "He's looking right this way."

The man said in a low voice, "Quick, open up, it's me, the Midnight Ghost."

Lydia and I were too scared to breathe.

The man repeated, "Open up! You know me! It's the Midnight Ghost!"

Lydia and I stayed where we were, our bare feet on the cold tile floor and our hearts pounding.

That's when we heard still more footsteps coming upstairs.

Lydia looked at me in horror, but this time I recognized my parents' steps.

"Quick," I said to Lydia, "back to bed or we'll really be in trouble!"

We pretended to be asleep when Mama came in. But just as she was about to leave my room, Lydia couldn't stand it anymore. She jumped up and said, "Oh, it's you! I thought it was Madam Eleven O'Clock!"

So I cried out to Papa, "Oh! The Midnight Ghost!"

Papa and Mama started to laugh.

"You little fakers!" said Mama. "You've been telling each other ghost stories again!"

But I insisted, "It's true! They really exist! Madam Eleven O'Clock and the Midnight Ghost are on the stairs!"

Papa and Mama looked worried. Papa said, "I'm going to see what's out there."

Moments later, he came back in with Madam Eleven O'Clock. She was deathly pale.

She nervously touched her star and said, "I don't want to bother you. I paid your neighbor to help me. But now he's not there. And I can't go back home, or the police will find me and take me away. It's already started. They're arresting everyone like me . . ." Then she added timidly, "I'm Mrs. Keller."

"Why did you say 'I'm Madam Eleven O'Clock' before?" I asked.

"Oh!" said Mrs. Keller. "It's a code name. Everyone your neighbor was supposed to help has one. A code with the time we're supposed to show up. But your neighbor is gone . . ."

Now I understood: "Midnight Ghost" was a code name, too. When he knocked at our door, he'd simply gotten the wrong apartment!

I said to Papa, "The Midnight Ghost is still on the stairs."

"No," Papa said. "No one's there. I'm sure. I looked."

So maybe the Midnight Ghost *was* a real ghost, since he had disappeared. I looked at Lydia to see what she thought of all this.

But Lydia wasn't looking at me. She was staring at the yellow star on Madam Eleven O'Clock's coat.

Suddenly she turned to Mama and said, "I'd like to go home."

I was shocked and thought Mama would say no and send her back to bed with me. After all, it was past midnight, and Lydia had been invited to my birthday party! But Mama only asked Papa, "What do you think?"

Lydia put on her jacket and said again, "I want to go home. Please take me home, right away."

We all stared at her. Timidly, Mrs. Keller said, "Perhaps you should warn her family."

Papa sighed, "So late at night? Well, maybe you're right. I'll take her home. Come on, Lydia, let's go."

That made me furious. I shouted at Lydia, "What's the matter with you? It's my birthday! You've forgotten all about it!"

Lydia seemed very embarrassed. She handed me a little package and said, "No, no, I haven't forgotten. Here's your present. I made it myself. I hope you like it." Then, without looking at me, she followed my father out the door. Mama gave her a kiss before she left. But I didn't.

I felt so angry, so hurt at being left by my best friend on my birthday that I
shouted at her from the top of the stairs, "I don't care! You're not my friend anymore!"

Why did I tell her she wasn't my friend, when I actually loved her so much? Sometimes you say things you don't really mean, things you're sorry about for a long time afterward. Now I'm old, and I still feel sorry about it.

Because I never saw Lydia again.

When Lydia left that night, Mama said to Madam Eleven O'Clock, "You can sleep in our daughter's bed. Tomorrow we'll see what we can do to help.

"And you," Mama said to me, "can sleep with Papa and me in the big bed."

I'd never been allowed to sleep with Mama and Papa before. Some pretty strange things were happening that night.

Papa soon returned home. "Well," he said, "that's that. I brought Lydia home and I warned her parents."

We all went to bed. I fell asleep cuddled up against Mama and Papa, completely worn out.

When I woke up, I instantly remembered that I was now nine years old.

Papa and Mama were already up. It was still pretty dark outside, but we could hear all kinds of noise from the street: people walking, shouts, whistles.

There was also a noise in the building. Someone was pounding on the door across from ours.

No one answered.

I ran to the hall, where Papa was standing. I was scared. I didn't know why, but I was.

Someone knocked on the door. Papa opened it. It was a French policeman, who asked, "Isn't anybody home across the hall?"

"No," Papa answered.

"That's not what they told us," the policeman grumbled.

He looked around our apartment, without really coming inside.

Madam Eleven O'Clock was still in my little bed, pretending to be asleep. From the doorway, the policeman could only see her hair spread out over the pillow.

"Ah!" he sighed, "how great to be young. These kids could sleep through an air raid!" And he went away.

Outside, the noise was getting louder.

People were filing by in a line, with suitcases in their hands. They were being watched over by French police. Why? They didn't look like robbers . . .

Suddenly I noticed that many of them were wearing yellow stars, like Lydia's.

Stars at morning, better take warning . . .

I felt my heart squeeze.

"Mama," I cried. "Where's Lydia?"

"Get dressed," Mama said. "We'll look for her."

I was ready in an instant. But we got there too late.

There wasn't anybody in her apartment. Their neighbors didn't know anything. Had Lydia's family been arrested? Had she escaped? There was no telling.

My throat felt tight. I said to Mama, "Lydia wasn't born under a lucky star."

Mama stopped walking. She looked at me and said forcefully, "Bad luck almost never comes from the stars above, Helen. And *this* bad luck certainly doesn't. Unfortunately, it comes from people, from the wickedness of some and the weakness of others. Sometimes it can be so hard to live together . . ."

She took me by the hand and we went back home.

Nobody was thinking about my birthday. Even I had forgotten about it.

Papa had taken Madam Eleven O'Clock somewhere safe. When he returned, I told him sadly, "Lydia's gone."

He sank down on the edge of the bed.

Mama said, "Maybe we shouldn't have brought her home."

Papa started to say, "Maybe we shouldn't have . . ." but he didn't finish his sentence.

We didn't know what to say, or what to do.

On my bed, I found the package that Lydia had given me. How I wished she was there to help me open it.

Inside was a cardboard doll that she'd cut out for me. For the head, she had glued on a photograph of her own face. She had made lots of clothes for the doll, too: dresses, blouses, shoes, and a little coat on which she had even drawn a star.

On the back of the doll, I wrote *Lydia.*

I waited and waited for Lydia to come back so I could tell her she was my best friend. But the war ended and still Lydia didn't come back. For a long time, I was angry at the stars.

Now I'm old. I only hope with all my heart that Lydia lived to become like me, a grandma, somewhere in the world.

Maybe one day she'll read this story to her granddaughter and she'll recognize herself in it and remember me. Then she'll call me on the telephone. "Hello, Helen?" she'll say. "It's me, Lydia."

It would make me so happy to hear her voice . . .

Stars at morning, better take warning.
Stars at night, hope is in sight.

I'll always have hope . . .